My Brother's Ghost

My Brother's Ghost

ALLAN AHLBERG

PUFFIN BOOKS

PUFFIN BOOKS

Published by the Penguin Group
Penguin Books Ltd, 80 Strand, London WC2R 0RL, England
Penguin Putnam Inc., 375 Hudson Street, New York, New York 10014, USA
Penguin Books Australia Ltd, 250 Camberwell Road, Camberwell, Victoria 3124, Australia
Penguin Books Canada Ltd, 10 Alcorn Avenue, Toronto, Ontario, Canada M4V 3B2
Penguin Books India (P) Ltd, 11 Community Centre, Panchsheel Park, New Delhi – 110 017, India
Penguin Books (NZ) Ltd, Cnr Rosedale and Airborne Roads, Albany, Auckland, New Zealand
Penguin Books (South Africa) (Pty) Ltd, 24 Sturdee Avenue, Rosebank 2196, South Africa

Penguin Books Ltd, Registered Offices: 80 Strand, London WC2R 0RL, England

www.penguin.com

First published by Viking 2000
Published in Puffin Books 2001

5

The moral right of the author has been asserted

Set in Cochin

Made and printed in England by Clays Ltd, St Ives plc

British Library Cataloguing in Publication Data
A CIP catalogue record for this book is available from the British Library

ISBN 0-141-30618-1

For Jessica

Contents

What I am about to tell you is true, well, as true as I can make it. (These things happened forty years ago.) Nothing is made up. Where I could not remember the details, I have left them out.

My name is Frances Fogarty. I am the middle child, the sister, in the story. Tom was my brother. Harry was, and happily still is, my brother.

Marge was my aunt, Rufus my dog, Rosalind my enemy. And so on.

You won't, I don't suppose, believe in ghosts. That can't be helped. The truth is, in a curious way I'm not sure I do either. Ghosts? I cannot speak for ghosts in general, numbers of ghosts. No . . . just the one.

The Funeral

H^{E WAS TEN WHEN} it happened, and I was nine and Harry was three. Running out into the street after Rufus, he was hit by nothing more than a silent, gliding milk-float. His head cracked down against the pavement edge. A fleck of blood rose up between his lips. His legs shook briefly, one heel rattling like a drumstick against the side of the float. And then he died.

My brother, my clever, understanding

older brother. My best friend and biggest pest of course sometimes. The sharer of my secrets, the buffer between me and Harry. Dead.

The milkman I remember was in tears, smashed bottles at his feet, milk running in the gutter. I had hold of Harry's hand. Rufus, all unconcerned, was still prancing about.

Four days later, the funeral. A pair of black cars, men in black suits, flowers and wreaths, the vicar. Harry and I were there. Uncle Stan said we should stay home. Auntie Marge said we should go. So we went.

It was a morning funeral. The grass in the cemetery was still wet with dew. The vicar spoke and the coffin was lowered on ropes into the ground. I remember then a train went by — invisibly in the cutting — the hiss and rattle of it, steam rising.

Who else was there besides us and Uncle Stan and Auntie Marge? The vicar, I've mentioned him. The undertaker's men. The grave diggers waiting at a distance. A neighbour, a friend of Auntie Marge's, had come I think, and the woman who ran the Cubs. The milkman too, perhaps. Somebody from the school.

And it was cold, I remember that, the low November sunlight glittering on the wet headstones. There was the sound of traffic from the road, the rumble of the presses in the nearby Creda factory.

It was Harry who saw him first. He grabbed my sleeve but said nothing. I looked ... and there was Tom. He had his hands in his pockets, his jacket collar up. His hair was as uncombed, as wild as ever. And he was leaning against a tree.

Looking for Tom

W E'D HAD OUR SHARE of troubles when Tom was alive. They did not go away after he died. Auntie Marge was softer with us for a day or two following the funeral. A bit of extra cake at teatime; a couple of comics at the weekend; now and then asking us how we were. But Harry was still wetting the bed, and soon she was yelling at him again as loud as ever and slapping the backs of his little legs. And I was yelling at her and getting clouted too.

And Uncle Stan was sloping off embarrassed to his shed. Things were back to normal.

Except of course for Tom.

We *had* seen him. At least Harry and I had. As we left the cemetery we had walked right past the tree where he was leaning. It was his face as clear as day. He looked at us, frowning, puzzled perhaps, as though our presence was a surprise to *him*. A little later, as the car drove away at a snail's pace, I saw him again, standing beside the grave. The grave diggers had removed the carpets of artificial grass, the platform of planks, and were shovelling the soil back into the hole. Tom was watching them.

School was hateful to me. I couldn't join in with things because of my leg. (Polio, I wore a caliper.) My teacher, Mrs Harris, said I was a scowler. (I was!) Rosalind and her gang were much of the time unfriendly, or worse. All the same, the day after the funeral I was back, only this time with no Tom to walk with or look out for me in the playground. Again, just as with Auntie Marge, there was a day or two of sympathetic smiles and considerate voices – Maureen Copper even shared her liquorice with me – before things got back to normal.

On Saturday I went looking for Tom. I had some errands to do for Auntie Marge in the morning. There was a steady drizzling rain in the early afternoon. So it was nearly four o'clock when I left the house. Rufus was with me, my excuse for going out.

The cemetery was divided into two parts, with a road, Cemetery Road, passing between them. I stood at the gates just after four. More rain was threatening. Already the street lights were beginning to glow. Rufus tugged us in. There was a light shining out from the side door of the chapel, I remember. Three or four people with flowers and cans of water were moving about. There was a smell of chrysanthemums.

What must I have been thinking then, as I stepped off down the path? I was only nine, after all. The cemetery was a place of morbid fears and dread. A place you avoided. A place you *ran* past (if you could).

Tom. I was thinking of Tom. I was scared and thinking of Tom. Holding Rufus close in on his lead for comfort and looking for Tom. Tom was here. He was here. *How* was he here?

The tree first, dripping noisily on its own dead leaves. No Tom. Then the grave: a mound of earth – drenched wreaths and flowers – smudgy, unreadable messages on little cards – muddy footprints in the grass. No Tom.

It was drizzling again now. My leg had begun to ache, the cold metal of the caliper chafing against my knee. Rufus was kicking his back legs in the loose soil. I turned and came away.

On Cemetery Road the street lights shone in the damp air, smudgily, like the blurry messages on the little cards. The air itself had a yellow, sulphurous tinge. (There were more coal fires and factory chimneys in those days.) A fog was beginning to form.

At the end of our street I let Rufus off his lead. He liked to run, to *hurtle* really, home from there. I limped on up to the house. On the low wall at the front enclosing a tiny patch of garden, Tom was sitting. His face still had that puzzled frowning look. His collar was still up.

I stood, my hair soaking wet and flat against my head, drops of water on my nose and ears and chin. Tom's mouth was open.

He was speaking or trying to, it seemed. There was no sound, as though a sheet of glass was placed between us. He made a gesture with his hand, a wave perhaps. There was a sharp tapping at the window. Auntie Marge was scowling at me, she was a scowler too. She wondered at me standing so still in the rain, wanted me in for my tea.

Tom watched me as I limped off down the entry. *His* hair, I just had time to notice, was bone dry.

Rufus

THAT NIGHT I TRIED to talk to Harry. I told him about Tom. That I had seen him again, here at the house. That Auntie Marge had not seen him. That when I got to the window straight after tea, he was no longer there. Harry said little. He wasn't talking much in those days anyway. 'No, no!' when Marge came after him. 'Milk,' sometimes to me at breakfast. And now, 'Tom – see Tom.' Harry's life I think at that time had just curled up into a ball. He was somewhere inside, sitting it out.

As soon as Harry was asleep, I crept out onto the landing and into Tom's room. Auntie Marge and Uncle Stan were downstairs with the radio on. Yellow foggy light from the street lamp lit up two thirds of the room and cast the rest into shadow. I stood uncertainly beside Tom's narrow bed. His things were all around me: Meccano models, balsa wood planes, his green Cubs' jumper with badges down the sleeves, marbles, cigarette cards . . . shoes. I sat on the bed and felt like an intruder.

I shivered. Already Tom's room was colder than the rest of the house and had begun to acquire that musty, unlived-in smell. A double-decker bus went sailing past the window. I sat there with my hands in my lap. Then the shapes in the room dissolved, and I began to cry.

The next day, Sunday, Harry and I went to Sunday school. We sang 'Ye Holy Angels Bright' and did a Bible quiz. I spent our collection money in Starkey's Sweet Shop. When we got home Auntie Marge smelled the sherbet on us, gave me a clout and sent the pair of us to our room. No tea, she said. No toys. Not a sound. Uncle Stan came in later, sheepishly, with a couple of biscuits. (Of course next morning she found the crumbs and *he* got a telling off.) The afternoon passed. It became darker in the room. (No light on.) Harry dozed off on his bed. I stood for a while at the window staring down into the yard. Presently, out came Rufus snuffling around, looking for amusement. I watched, and suddenly there was Tom. He was following Rufus here and there across the yard. Rufus had hold of an old deflated ball and was shaking it like a rat. Tom held out a hand, crouched down beside him, attempted to ruffle his furry neck. And Rufus, dim *unseeing* Rufus, no sixth sense (hardly five), went bounding through him.

Bad Times

I WILL SAY SOMETHING here about polio. It is not, after all and thank goodness, a disease that any of us has cause to fear these days. But in those days . . . well, there were two others in my school with calipers on their legs. There was also a boy, I seem to remember, who had it and was so ill he just stayed home.

Polio – poliomyelitis – is a virus. One of its many unpleasant effects is to paralyse certain muscles. You needed then to wear a metal and leather brace, a 'caliper' as it was called. This helped your weakened leg (or legs) to support your weight. I had caught polio when I was six and had been wearing a caliper for about a year and a half.

Rosalind Phipps was just a nasty child, I can see this now. Though maybe she had her troubles too. (What went on in *her* house, I wonder.) She was a bully to me, she and her spiteful gang. 'Frances Frogarty,' they would chant in their sarcastic sing-song voices. It drove me crazy. I had a temper. I would rise to the bait and Rosalind knew it. Then having got me all worked up she would somehow cunningly duck out of sight, leaving me to suffer the consequences with Mrs Harris, Mr Cork or whoever. Also she would say bad things about Harry (her little sister and Harry went to the same nursery), or worse about our parents. 'You only live with your Auntie!' I wanted to punch her.

So I was having a bad time at school and Harry and I were having a bad time at home. Auntie Marge had no interest in children, no maternal instincts I heard her say on one occasion. When Tom was around he often managed to deflect her anger. Without him we were horribly exposed. She was impatient, humourless, cruel.

The following week, the week after the funeral, it snowed for the first time. Harry stood in wonder at the bedroom window. 'Snow,' he whispered. He had woken me up to see it. My enthusiasm was less than his. I was thinking more of the ice that would surely follow, the slippery pavements, my clumsy leg.

At eight o'clock in came Marge in her blackest mood. She threw the blankets back from Harry's bed, wrinkled her nose and yelled. (He was on my bed already, behind me.) 'I'm sick of this!' She snatched the wet sheet from the bed and the rubber sheet beneath and hurled them to the floor. 'Sick, sick, sick!'

Two nights later I woke in the half light, the curtains partly open, a clear sky, a moon, light bouncing up from the frosty snow. Harry was stumbling out of bed, feeling his way with Tom beside him. They left the room. I followed. The lino beneath my feet was freezing. The clock downstairs struck twice. I could hear Rufus groaning in his sleep.

I found Harry in the bathroom, his pyjama trousers around his feet, having a sleepwalking wee. Tom was there. Somehow I knew better than to interfere. Tom glanced at me over his shoulder. He had a hand on Harry's shoulder. (Could Harry feel it?)

I left. Minutes later Harry came back to bed, his eyes half shut, alone. I fell asleep then and dreamt my usual dream or one of them. Mum and I were at the seaside tucking our dresses into our knickers, splashing in the waves. Dad was in the distance . . . calling.

The next night Tom came again, and the next and the next. He arrived at different times: twelve-thirty, two o'clock, three. He got Harry up, or Harry got himself up, and led him to the bathroom. Each night Harry had a wee. Each morning Harry's bed was dry.

I struggled to make sense of what was happening. Tom was taking Harry to the toilet. How did he accomplish this? Could Harry feel Tom's hand upon his shoulder? (Rufus after all had leapt straight through him.) Could Tom *communicate* with Harry?

Was Harry hearing more than I was? For I was hearing nothing, not a sound. On that second night, for instance, Tom returned to the bedroom and stood at the window. The moonlight caught his springy tousled hair. His collar was still up. Harry had dropped straight back into sleep. I sat up in bed and called Tom's name, an urgent whisper. 'Tom? Tom!' He turned to face me. Once more his mouth was open. He spoke, or tried to. Once more the plate of glass between us. No sound.

But the next night there was a sound, though one I'd rather not have heard. It was a slow growling sound, like something played at the wrong speed. 'Frr.' For the first time, I remember, I was really afraid. I pulled the bedclothes over my head and held my breath. 'Frr.' When I peeped out later, Tom was gone.

The thing is, it was Tom who was making

this awful noise, all the while with a serious, almost hopeful look in his eyes as though he expected *me* to understand it. Well, I believe I may have sensed something then or begun to. It *was* my brother I was hearing, seeing – yes of course my brother, my loving brother, my graceful, quiet, clever brother. But then again, not quite my brother now. It was my brother's ghost.

The Fight

I T'S OCCURRED TO ME (just now, as I write) that really so far I have not described exactly what it was that Harry and I *saw* when we saw Tom. The main thing is, you see, Tom was never transparent or wispy like the ghosts you sometimes get in the movies. He was no apparition. You might walk through him, but you couldn't see through him. (At least, we couldn't. Others it seems couldn't see him at all.) So you could say the way he looked to us was completely normal. The only exception to this was sudden movement, quick changes of direction. At such times Tom's outline, the edges of him, would quiver and blur like a swimmer under water or someone seen in the distance through a heat haze.

Mrs Harris was an average sort of teacher. She did her best for me, I suppose, though I was not among her favourites. I was a prickly child altogether. I had no winning ways. Consequently, when the fight happened it was hardly a surprise to me when Mrs Harris took the wrong side, blamed the wrong person.

It was December now, Christmas and my birthday approaching. We decorated the classroom with silver paper chains and cotton wool snowmen. Mrs Harris brought some twigs of holly from her own garden. We made cards for our mums and dads, or, added Mrs Harris hastily, our grandmas, cousins, aunties – anybody really. I made mine for Harry.

In the last week of the term we had a Christmas dinner in the hall. Some of the teachers joined in wearing party hats. Bad luck brought me to Rosalind's table.

I was not in the best of moods to begin with. Auntie Marge had had a go at us that morning about something or other. Tom had not been near us for two or three days. My leg was aching. So whatever it was that Rosalind said or did – it *was* something – I was ready for her. I pushed her off her chair. A bowl of Christmas pudding and custard followed her to the floor. She aimed a sly kick at me, and I fell on her.

There was a satisfying whoosh of air from

Rosalind. My heavy calipered leg was a help too on this occasion. I would surely have punched my enemy then. I would have bitten her. But Mrs Harris in her crooked party hat dragged me away.

The following morning Tom walked with me to school. On the way, at the corner of Seymour Road and Tugg Street, he completed his first spoken word. 'Frr . . . ances,' he said.

Remembering

M Y MEMORIES OF WHAT happened to us all those years ago are unreliable at times, obliterated even. But I remember that first walk with Tom completely. Every detail. It's like a film in my head.

I remember the glistening blue-brick pavement, the rusty railings and the ivy outside the Rolfe Street Baptist Chapel, the belching smoke from one of old man Cutler's allotment bonfires. I remember him too, in his off-white painter's overalls and his pork pie hat, poking at it. I remember colliding with Herbie, the bread man, in the first shock of seeing Tom. I remember the pleasure and relief in Tom's face when he got that first word – my name! – out. Above all, though, I remember my feelings.

I felt so happy and sad . . . and strange. Tom just appeared, you see. (I nearly said, 'out of nowhere'.) He spoke, only the one word. And then he simply walked beside me as he had ever used to.

What a curious experience, to walk to school with a ghost. How odd I must have seemed, glancing sideways, dodging unnecessarily, smiling into the thin air. I was looking out for Tom. It distressed me when someone went blundering through him. But he – out of habit? – was avoiding them anyway. So it rarely happened. I felt no urge to talk yet, to interrogate him. (Where had he been?) Mainly, I believe, I was just so glad of his company. Going to school with Tom, entering the playground with Tom, merely knowing he was present in the building, had always helped me in the past. It was helping me now.

Tom and I joined the cluster of parents and children at the school crossing. I studied Tom out of the corner of my eye. He was studying me. Both of us smiled. It came into my mind then how strange all of this must be for *him*. And then I had another thought: *he was working it out.*

Years before, back in the days when we were a family, I recall Tom brought a maths book home. He was clever at maths, could do most of it in his head and simply put the answers down. Anyway, on this occasion his teacher had written in the margin next to an especially complicated sum that Tom had got right, 'How did you get this answer?' And Tom in the tiniest writing had replied:

'I worked it out!'

This became a joke in our family for quite a while, a catchphrase even. How did you . . .? I worked it out.

The school bell was ringing. Mr Hawkins was out on the forecourt shovelling coke down the chute into his boiler room. Tom stopped to watch. Rosalind, Amanda and the others were hanging around at the school gates. I observed a satisfying-looking bruise on Rosalind's leg, a wary look in her eye. I walked straight past them.

Canada

THE WEEKS AND MONTHS went by, Christmas and my birthday with them. For a while the circumstances of our lives improved. Harry was no longer wetting the bed at all. He had also now begun to talk more, run around more. He played in the yard, when the weather permitted, with a little friend he'd made at the nursery. And I got invited to a party! What sort of party or who invited me, I'm ashamed to say I have forgotten. But I remember the dress. And I remember Auntie Marge taking me out one Saturday morning to Haywoods Outfitters to buy it.

Marge *was* a terror, but not all the time. She had her better side too. She was a hard worker, cleaning other people's houses in the daytime and offices at night. Much of her wages I'm sure were spent on us. Also, although she did yell at us and hit us, she was often truly sorry for it later. She would come up to our room sometimes with tears in her eyes and attempt to cuddle us, offer us little treats.

One more improvement: I had begun having physiotherapy for my polio-stricken leg, exercises to strengthen the wasted muscle. In time, it was suggested, I might have the caliper removed, stand and walk unaided.

Actually, I have a confession to make about this leg. When I began my story, I had half a mind not to mention it, write myself a pair of normal legs, as it were. It was partly Harry's idea. (He has been reading my manuscript as I write it.) In his opinion the leg is just too much: no mum, no dad, no brother, a wicked auntie and to cap it all a pathetic poor old *limping* leg. Like Tiny Tim. Unbelievable! (according to Harry).

Well, I do want you to believe it of course, despite what I said at the beginning. And it does seem rather ridiculous now, all those heaped-up troubles (and more to come) – like Job in the Bible. The leg's too much, says Harry. Well, it was too much, I suppose, for me at times. I was hugely sick of it and often wished it gone. But it is a part of the truth, a part of me (Ha!), so I have kept it in.

Meanwhile, what about Tom? Tom came and went. He talked more too, in his new-found gravelly voice – haltingly, long effort-filled pauses, silences. He talked in our room at night, in the park beside me walking Rufus, in the cemetery even on one occasion, with Auntie Marge close by putting flowers on *his* grave. He talked to me, and to Harry sometimes . . . and to Rufus.

Rufus, you see, had really been more Tom's dog than mine. Tom couldn't give up trying to get through to him. I can see him now, crouching beside that little heedless dog or racing after him across the football pitches. Tom made light of his rejections. 'Bad dog . . . Rufus!' he'd say when Rufus ignored him for the umpteenth time. But you could tell he wasn't happy about it. It's an odd thing, but I almost think that watching Tom with Rufus on those occasions was more unbearable than all of it. Tears would come to my eyes and I would feel Tom's loss – my loss of him, his of Rufus. Yes.

Then at the beginning of March, a flurry of events. Auntie Marge scalded her arm slightly in the steam from a boiling pan. Rufus sneaked his way into the front room and attacked the padded seat of one of Marge's favourite chairs, chewed it up almost altogether. And Uncle Stan lost his job.

The lost job was the most significant thing of course, but it was Rufus that triggered the explosion. Marge went berserk. She chased poor Rufus round the kitchen with a broom and then with a clothes line, lashing at him as he cowered under the table. Harry quivered in a corner. Tom stood powerlessly by. I threw a fit.

I rushed at Marge and pushed her violently in the small of the back. (I could not bear the terrible guilt-stricken look in Rufus's eyes.) She toppled sideways and brought a cut glass vase – another favourite – crashing to the floor. She screamed – swore, in fact – and turned on me. I bolted through the kitchen door and ran, Rufus ahead of me.

Things were back again to normal.

That night I lay in bed unable to sleep. Harry was sleeping. Rufus was chained up in the yard below, whining; you could just hear him. Tom was somewhere else.

Eventually I got up and crept onto the landing. A glow of light rising from the rooms below. Voices and clinking cups. Auntie Marge was doing most of the talking. She sounded calm. Stan spoke now and then. I could not make out much of what was said, and yet I felt a sudden clutch of fear. This was the first time, I am fairly sure, that *Canada* was mentioned.

Ghost Talk

THERE IS A WAY in which with time we can take anything for granted. The strange becomes familiar, the extraordinary ordinary. As the year moved on, winter into spring, Tom's involvement with us, his presence in our lives (our presence in his death?) became what we expected, what we were used to. Normal. The mystery and the matter-of-factness were one and the same. We told no one, by the way, not a soul. The secret was ours.

Yet periodically it would come upon me how bewildering, how unfathomably odd it all was. Here was Tom, my dear dead brother, leaning over Harry's bed perhaps, or sitting beside me on a park bench, his eternal jacket collar up, smiling, frowning. And yet if I were just to reach out (which I never did), put my hand upon his arm . . .

How can I convey the strangeness of him? He was so like his previous self, but then . . . There was the rasp and graininess of his new voice, the almost imperceptible peculiarities in his appearance. No motion, no wind in his unruly hair, no rain on his face, only that curious shimmering, shivering at the edges of him when he ran. No actual contact either, with the tree he was supposedly leaning against; the pavement, floor, grass on which he apparently stood. He was here and with us, and elsewhere.

Elsewhere; that was a conundrum too. I

came to believe that Tom was like some kind of mobile light bulb, moving himself here and there, switching himself on and off. Except he couldn't always find the switch and had no map. Tom was bewildered too. He compared his condition once to a kind of dreaming. The logic of normal life did not apply. When he wasn't 'somewhere' – usually that meant with me and Harry – he had no memories at all. Then sometimes, randomly, he'd find himself stood watching a football match on Barnford Hill or boys fishing in the Tipton canal. Once he even got as far as Dudley Zoo; a keeper with his bucket, thrown fish in the air, the glazed and playful seals.

Tom's talk: another conundrum. I wish you could have heard it; the telegram sentences, out-of-step remarks, huge silences. There was not much conversation, that was for sure. He rarely answered questions directly, though something might emerge days or even weeks later. Talking to Tom was a tennis match with few rallies. But at least in time the tension in his speech relaxed, the production of the words themselves was less of a strain. Tom would utter the most perplexing, unconnected thoughts serenely.

Yet consider too what he achieved. Out of his ghostly maze he somehow made his way. He got to Harry when he was needed. And he got to me.

The Thief

I T WAS MAY NOW. Tom had recently seen the seals and over a spread of three or four days told me about them. (Stan surprised me in the kitchen on one of these occasions, talking to myself apparently, and gave me a funny look.) Harry had the measles, Rosalind too incidentally. Rufus was wilder than ever and had got his ear chewed up in a fight. And I was taking sixpences from Marge's Christmas jar.

Stealing. Yes, you would have to say it was. And yet . . . Marge, you see, was strict about most things. Jobs, for instance. You got pocket money but you did jobs for it. Even Harry had jobs. Well, I was doing the jobs and she, quite often, for no reason in my opinion, was stopping my pocket money. So I was paying myself what I was owed, give or take a sixpence.

Stan, though, had no job. He spent much time in his shed, making shelves and a bathroom cabinet. He helped out on a friend's allotment and got paid in cabbages and such. He walked Rufus all over the Rounds Green Hills till even the dog had had enough.

Canada had some connection with Stan's unemployment, I knew that much. Stan had cousins in Toronto. Letters with Canadian stamps would arrive from time to time. But lately there had been a rush of them.

Conversations with hints of Canada — Toronto, dollars, cousin Ruth — would fade into silence when I entered the room. One day Uncle Stan (in his best suit) and Auntie Marge took the train to London, leaving us with our neighbour, Shirley. They did not return till after dark. I heard Canada again from my listening post at the top of the stairs.

Then, the inevitable: Marge found out about the sixpences, caught me red-handed in fact. (I looked as guilty as Rufus.) She of course erupted. I was a bad girl, a wicked girl altogether. A little thief. Ungrateful. After all she'd done. She was just sick of me, sick of this whole place — street, town, country! — and would be glad to leave.

Now out it all came. Canada. That was the place, she said, for her and Stan anyway. But not for me, no. No thieves wanted in

Canada. I would stay right here (no mention of Harry). 'Yes . . . see if they'll have you in Caldicott Road!'

All this happened one Wednesday afternoon in the half-term holiday. Harry was at his friend's house, Stan out with Rufus. I ended up in my room; Marge was banging around downstairs. I sat on my bed and scowled at the grey, rain-spattered window. I pulled my tin box out from under the bed and opened it. I spread its contents on the floor, took up a bracelet and put it on.

Tom was beside me, kneeling. He stretched out a hand towards a tattered envelope with photographs in it. 'Black,' he said. The rain came rattling harder against the glass. Downstairs I heard a door slam, Rufus barking. 'Pool,' said Tom.

Important Things

'BLACKPOOL,' TOM HAD SAID, and I knew what he wanted. I removed a photograph from the envelope. It was smaller than the rest, black and white. It showed a skinny boy with wet hair in swimming trunks shading his eyes from the sun. Beside him a smaller scowling girl, barefoot in a sundress. On the back was written in our mother's hand:

'Thomas and Frances
Blackpool 1952.'

43

This battered green tin box was my consolation, Tom's too at times. It contained my important things: a little turquoise bracelet, present from Mum, a Japanese fan that Dad had brought back from his travels, a tiny yellowing paper plane that he had made, a brooch with Grandma's photo in it. And so on. The box itself had belonged to my dad. It had his initials, R.F.F., painted in white letters on the side.

Once there had been four of us, you see. Our dad had been a soldier. He died in the Korean war in 1953. Five months later Mum died giving birth to Harry. After the funeral we moved down to the Midlands and came to live with Marge and Stan. Yes, once there had been four of us, then three, then briefly four again, then three again . . . now two.

I fell asleep, dozed off on the bed though it was still light outside, Harry not yet back from his friend's. I had the dream again, the familiar simple mystifying dream. We're on the beach. Dad's in the water, swimming, waving. Mum's in a deckchair fast asleep. Tom is missing from the scene. I'm running from a distance, anxious.

Running Away

CANADA WAS BAD NEWS. Caldicott Road was worse. In that town in those days misbehaving children were commonly threatened with two unpleasant possibilities. One was the rag-and-bone man, the other Caldicott Road. Caldicott Road was a children's home. I had *been* in a children's home once before, after Mum died and before Marge and Stan came up to fetch us. I remembered the experience too well: awful food, lumpy beds, a disinfected unhomely smell, the sense of being abandoned.

It was eight o'clock that same evening. Marge was out cleaning offices. Stan had nipped round to the allotments for half an hour. Harry and I were supposedly in bed.

I packed two bags, one for Harry. I had explained to him that we were going to visit Auntie Annie. Annie was our other auntie, the one we almost never saw. She and Marge weren't speaking. (It's just occurred to me, she would have been at Tom's funeral too. What else have I forgotten?)

Tom appeared as we were getting our coats on, his face serious and frowning. 'Not,' he said. And some time later, 'go!' But we were going anyway. I was worked up, frantic and afraid. Stan might come back at any minute. I was defiant too, another handful of sixpences in my pocket.

'Stay!' said Tom. He was in the hallway

now, his arms out wide as though to stop us. We squeezed past him.

Harry and I left the house, left Rufus too, chained up in the yard. (He'd been chewing again.) I could not take Rufus, I needed both hands for the bags and Harry.

Tom pursued us for a time down the street till suddenly he was no longer there. The street lamps had begun to glow. Dark masses of cloud hung in the sky before us. I hurried Harry along. Auntie Annie lived out on the Wolverhampton Road. I thought that we could find our way there, hoped we could. But this journey of course had more to do with leaving than arriving.

In Tugg Street we met Mrs Starkey on the steps of her shop, putting up her umbrella. Spots of rain had begun to fall.

'Hallo, dearies – you're out late!'

Harry started on about Auntie Annie but

I kept him moving. The rain fell heavier. We took shelter in the paper shop doorway. Harry was getting restless. For a time we stood just staring out into the glistening empty street. A dog came trotting purposefully along; a man went by on a motorbike. Light shone from the windows of the houses. There was the faintest sound of a piano playing.

The rain eased. I popped a peardrop into Harry's mouth and on we went.

I have a good memory – you will have noticed! – especially for those days. (As we get older, a brighter light, it seems, illuminates our childhood.) I can remember such details of our running away that it startles *me*. A small cat glowering at us from the bottom of a privet hedge. Harry spotting a penny on the pavement outside the chip shop and stooping to pick it up. Tiny hopping frogs on the towpath of the canal.

The canal, yes, I remember the canal. But the next bit is not so clear, not clear at all. It was a short cut, you see, between two bridges, one road and another. It was well-lit from the lights in a nearby factory car park. We went along the towpath (I remember more slowly now. Harry had begun to flag, my leg was aching. The frogs hopped out. Some plopped into the water, I suppose. Harry maybe crouched to see them. But was I in front of him then or behind? Did I crouch too? Was it the slippery ground that did it or my weak leg sliding away beneath me? Or both? Or neither? Well, whatever it was it hardly matters now. What happened was, I fell into the canal.

Drowning

IT TAKES MORE TIME to drown than you would think. There's time, for instance, after your fight with the water is lost, to experience many things. To begin with, though, there's simply panic and shock. I may have slid into that canal like a canoe with barely a ripple, but there were ripples now and waves. I was thrashing and whirling about, desperate to regain the bank, and sinking.

The water was cold, foul-smelling,

covered in scum. I disappeared beneath it. There was a pounding in my head, bright fractured light behind my eyes. I sank.

And rose again. I was coughing and spluttering. Slime and bits of weed were clinging to my hair and face. I sucked more air into my lungs and swallowed water. I sank again.

I was so weighted down, you see: my waterlogged clothes and shoes, my bag still over my shoulder, my heavy calipered leg, the stolen sixpences even.

The heaviness was winning. My struggles ceased. Time expanded.

I saw in quick and flickering succession, inside my flooded head, the image of Harry on the bank – poor Harry – poor, orphaned Harry (then there was *one*). And Dad, his mouth all comically puckered up, teaching me to whistle. And Dora, my tiny one-armed Bakelite doll. I saw Mrs Harris on a stepladder hanging paper chains. Leaping Rufus. A patch of sunlit sky. A little boat at sea. I saw my mother buttering bread. I saw Tom.

I saw Tom. I *did* see Tom. He was there in the water with me. And shouting (in the water, *under* it).

'Swim, Fran, swim!'

But Tom must know I couldn't swim, even without this . . . heaviness.

'Fran!'

Tom's gravelly voice was a shock in my ear. My drifting foot grazed the bottom or, more likely, some submerged pram or other bit of rubbish. I tensed my leg, kicked and rose again. One final effort. My head broke the surface.

'Yell, Frances!' Tom shouted. 'Yell, yell, YELL!'

I rolled upon my back for a second and glimpsed the blue-black sky. And yelled.

The Hospital

I WAS RESCUED FROM the waters of the Tipton canal by thirty-seven-year-old Mr Arthur Finch, a self-employed carpenter of 109 Brass House Lane, West Bromwich. (I have confidence in these details. I still have the newspaper cutting.) Apparently Harry had raced back up onto the bridge seeking help. Meanwhile Mr Finch had come along the towpath on his bike, heard my cries and dived in fully clothed. His wife, Mrs Muriel Finch, was reported as being unsurprised by her husband's behaviour. He was always a hero in her eyes, she said.

One other thing, while I remember: Mr Finch, having got me onto the towpath, dived in again, convinced as he was that someone else was in there. He had heard *two* voices, you see.

I experienced nothing of the rescue itself, being unconscious even before my saviour reached me. (Those yells were literally my last gasp.) When I came round some hours later, I was in a hospital bed. The ward was dark, with pools and patches of light, green and yellow walls, two rows of beds along its length.

I lay quite still, staring up at the ceiling. After a time I noticed a huddled figure at the side of the bed. It was Marge, fast asleep with her glasses askew and her handbag in her lap. The bed felt cool, the sheets stretched taut like the sails of a ship, the pillow thin and hard. A baby was crying somewhere. There was the sharp sour smell of disinfectant. I drifted off.

Dreaming. And in my dream I was drowning again, only this time in the sea. And Dad and Harry were looking for me, up and down the beach. And I was there. There! But they never saw me.

I woke again. Streaks of grey and pinkish light at the windows. Marge's seat was vacant. A nurse passed down the centre aisle carrying a tray. Tom was watching me from the end of the bed.

Tom, my other rescuer (no place for him, though, in the *Warley Weekly News*). He moved and stood beside me. Smiled, leant over, and put his hand on mine.

I felt it – did I? I did, though half asleep and woozy from the medicine they'd given me. It wasn't much of a touch, hardly 'substantial', more like the flimsiest, frailest piece of cloth falling on you; a feeling of graininess, texture. Not much, but something, surely, more than mere empty air.

The nurse came back and approached the bed. She stood where Tom was standing, took my pulse. Tom moved aside. He watched the nurse, waiting for her to leave. He gazed out of one of the rapidly brightening windows. He turned his collar down.

Getting Better

I WAS EXTREMELY ILL for a while, detained in the hospital for nearly three weeks. The swallowed water was responsible. I caught some kind of fever from it. That Tipton canal almost did for me twice over, you might say. But then I began to get well. Marge and Stan, and Harry too, came every evening to see me. Mrs Harris came with a basket of fruit. Later on she came again with a copy of *Black Beauty* that all the children in the school, she said, had clubbed together to buy. I seem to remember she brought two or three children with her. (I still have the book.)

Then what? Out of the hospital, back to home and school. Before I knew it, it was the summer holidays. Marge and Stan took us on a train to Weston-super-Mare. We stayed in a caravan. I'm not sure where they got the money from; Stan was still out of a job.

Speaking of money, those sixpences, the ones I took for running away with, were never mentioned. I've always wondered, did Marge most likely find them in my pocket, or had they disappeared into the canal? Are they there still, sunken treasure? Who knows.

Something else that was never mentioned was Canada. Odd letters still arrived but otherwise it just fell out of the conversation. I never knew why. Then in the autumn Stan got a job.

I guess we couldn't know it at the time, but all that business with the canal, the fever and so on was to prove the lowest point not just for me but for the others too. The curve of all our lives after that more or less went up.

So Stan got a job, and a good one, at Guest, Keen and Nettlefolds. A month or so later, with Christmas approaching, we moved into a new house, a council semi, with a garden all to itself backing onto the park. Spring came. Stan acquired a small greenhouse, Harry and I had our own little plots and Rufus took great delight in the prospect of the park, his absolutely favourite place for a walk.

In the summer it was Marge's turn for a new job. She gave up cleaning and went to work in a shop. Marge, I suspect I may have been too hard on Marge. Anyway, she improved. Her temper was still uncertain. She yelled at us at times but never hit us again. We became less afraid of her. Once she threw a teacup straight through the (closed) kitchen window for some reason or other – not at us, not at anybody. After which, appalled by her own action, she looked at me and both of us burst out laughing. (I could hardly ever remember Marge laughing before.)

As for Tom, he was his usual unusual self. He found his way to our new house, spent time with me and Harry in our now separate rooms, accompanied us to school. He disappeared too, sometimes for a whole week. On one occasion he found himself in the Plaza cinema in Brierley Hill watching a war movie. On another he spent the entire day at a cricket match, Warwickshire versus Surrey. Tom was not even interested in cricket.

❊

Then, in the spring of 1958, surprising news: I'd passed the Eleven Plus (the entrance exam for the local grammar school). I was, it turned out, cleverer than we knew. Mrs Harris was flabbergasted. Rosalind likewise, although she also passed. Marge went mad . . . with delight. She it was who first read the letter and yelled to Stan about it and hurtled (yelling) up the stairs to me. Marge, I never thought to see the day, was proud of me.

That morning I went to school with a glow on my cheeks and my Eleven Plus letter in my hand. Tom walked beside me. It was then that for the very first time I noticed it:

I was taller than him.

Tom's Compass

H E WAS TEN WHEN it happened, and I was nine and Harry was three. Now I was eleven and Harry was five and Tom was still ten. (Keep going: at the time of writing, I am fifty-two – good grief! – Harry is forty-six and Tom, wherever he is, is ten.)

That's how it was. That's what being a ghost, Tom discovered, was all about, or partly about. (He of course had noticed what was happening long before we did.)

So the years passed and we moved

on and Tom stayed where he was, marooned. His appearance never changed, not one unruly hair on his head. His voice, though, modulated somewhat in time to a lighter, more normal pitch, either that or I just got used to it. His conversation became even quirkier, like random bits of a jigsaw puzzle or peculiar crossword clues. He would disappear now, often for weeks on end, and then show up looking dazed. He rarely spoke of his ghost life. Questions about it appeared unsettling to him. We gave up asking them.

I worried about him. He seemed so much smaller with the years, frailer, sadder. I wanted to help but never found the means. There again, how hard it is sometimes to capture the truth. For Tom was also funny and relaxed. It amused him to have this huge and hulking little sister, this giant of a baby brother. And he watched out for us still, charted his course to intersect our lives. He had no map perhaps, but he had a compass.

When I was thirteen, I had my caliper removed and replaced by a special shoe (a thicker sole and heel). Marge became manageress of the shop she worked in. At fourteen I started going out with Roger Horsfield, my first boyfriend. Harry, now nine and soon to be the tallest of us all, was playing football every evening in the park. He was a prodigy already and later was to play for West Bromwich Albion reserves.

Rufus was by this time an elderly dog. He stumbled around, not seeing very well. The furniture was safe with him.

When I was fifteen, Rufus died.

Leaving

So here I sit forty years on writing all this down. It's late afternoon, October, a sudden sharpness in the air, red-golden leaves out on the lawn, my dear cat, Muggs, prowling the shrubbery.

And I begin to wonder, did these things happen? Did I see them, hear them, smell them? Have I *remembered* it, all of it, truly, as it really was? Is nothing made up?

I don't know. Harry, I mentioned earlier, has been reading what I've written and he confirms the gist of it. (But he was only three when it began.) Memories of course are insubstantial (like ghosts!). There again, things are real, and I still have my box. It's here beside me on the table as I write: the bracelet, the newspaper cutting, Tom's cigarette cards. And when I hold these items in my hand and spread them out . . . and smell them, I feel a rush of pure conviction. My doubts dissolve.

We buried Rufus in the garden, Harry and I. It was quite early in the morning. We agreed a spot with Stan and dug the hole. Rufus's little body was stiff already. (Rufus was a mongrel terrier, I don't believe I ever mentioned that.) He looked so normal, lying on his side, his stubby tail, the grey hair round his muzzle, his one brown-circled eye. We covered him over, patted the soil into place.

Rufus's ghost showed up in the garden on the following afternoon. I saw him from the kitchen window. There was only me in the house. I ran outside. It was midsummer, a hot and cloudless day. Rufus staggered towards me. I knelt and held out a hand. It was of course no use. Rufus blundered on and through me. His water bowl was still in its place outside the kitchen door. Poor Rufus reached the bowl, butted his head down into it and lapped vainly at the puddle of water it contained. After a while he gave up. Moments later, with a terrible slowed-down grinding sort of sound, Rufus barked.

For two days Rufus continued to appear before us (Harry and me), almost always in the garden. He was a pitiful sight: slow, stumbling, bewildered. He could not fathom his new relationship to people and things.

He kept trying to make contact. On the evening of the third day, Tom arrived.

Rufus was lying on the little patch of slabs outside the kitchen door. Tom came up to him, knelt down and *ruffled his fur*. I saw the fur move. Rufus rolled over and almost managed a leap. He collided joyfully with Tom. I saw the impact. He licked Tom's hand. I saw the shine of his saliva on Tom's skin.

Tom took Rufus's lead out of his pocket; a ghostly lead for a ghostly dog. (Had it been there all those years?) Rufus quivered as he'd always done at the prospect of a walk. Tom gave me a smile and a wave. He led Rufus away, across the garden, through the fence and into the trees. A kite was dipping and swinging above them in the sky; distant children shouting in the park.

We never saw Tom again (or Rufus), though we looked for him on and off for years. My brother's ghost is gone and it's all for the best. He's somewhere (that's the most you can say), has Rufus with him, and is working it out.